FIRST STORY
CHANGING LIVES THROUGH WRITING

There is dignity and power in telling our own story. We help young people find their voices.

First Story places professional writers into secondary schools serving low-income communities, where they work intensively with students and teachers to foster confidence, creativity and writing ability.

Our programmes expand young people's horizons and raise aspirations. Students gain vital skills that underpin their success in school and support their transition to further education and employment.

To find out more and get involved, go to
www.firststory.org.uk.

First Story is a registered charity number 1122939 and a private company limited by guarantee incorporated in England with number 06487410. First Story is a business name of First Story Limited.

First published 2021 by First Story Limited
44 Webber Street, Southbank, London, SE1 8QW

www.firststory.org.uk

ISBN 978-0-85748-495-6

1 3 5 7 9 10 8 6 4 2

A CIP catalogue record for this book is available from the British Library.

Printed and bound in the UK by Aquatint
Typeset by Avon DataSet Ltd
Copyedited by Camille Ralphs
Proofread by Alison Key
Cover designed by Julie Ann Monks (https://www.julieannmonks.com/)

Outpost 8

An Anthology by the First Story Group
at Longcroft School and Sixth Form College

EDITED BY LEE HARRISON | 2021

FIRST STORY
CHANGING LIVES THROUGH WRITING

As Patron of First Story I am delighted that it continues to foster and inspire the creativity and talent of young people in secondary schools serving low-income communities.

I firmly believe that nurturing a passion for reading and writing is vital to the health of our country. I am therefore greatly encouraged to know that young people in this school – and across the country – have been meeting each week throughout the year in order to write together.

I send my warmest congratulations to everybody who is published in this anthology.

Camilla

HRH The Duchess of Cornwall

Contents

Introduction

Lee Harrison, Writer-in-Residence

Isolation is something we know a bit too much about these days. As the world changes beyond recognition, we find ourselves in a kind of outpost on the frontier of a strange land. As we sit in this bunker between worlds, trying to make sense of it all, we're forced to wonder – what was the world like before, and how would we like it to be in the future?

It is a strange effect of isolation that being separated from one world can push you together with another, where safe, once-familiar places become enmeshed with strange and foreign lands, and the boundaries between the real and the imagined become blurred. This place, we call *Outpost 8*.

I had the daunting task of following on from Longcroft School's impressive debut year with First Story, and a very large, very lively bunch of Year 8s to work with. At its core, with many of them raised in military families, this group knew how it felt to be posted, on the move, in transition amidst uncertain times. A touch of hesitation about putting themselves *out there* was only to be expected, but with the knowledge that these are the very times when we need to find our voices – and with a *bit* of encouragement – they surely spoke.

This group brought an experience of loss and gain and triumph that perhaps went beyond its years. They met their tasks with the kind of honesty that defines a good First Story experience – bringing not so much the fancy words, but the true words, words that could only come from these particular humans. And you will find – even among some of the more surreal inventions – that there is an invigorating, sometimes tragic, sometimes joyous, sometimes brutal honesty to the words contained in this anthology.

Longcroft School is proving itself something of a hotbed of literary and artistic talent, as this year's writing competitions demonstrate. I was impressed with the wider school entries for First Story's very first EcoPoetry Competition, one of which won a runner-up prize. And not only that – for the second year running, a Longcroft writer won the national 100-Word Story Competition! I salute these winning entries, and proudly recruit them to our outpost.

I would like to thank Ms Carvill, the field marshal who did so much to enable the whole campaign. Throughout it all, she has been genuinely dedicated to giving the young writers a chance to express themselves. It's reassuring to know that there are champions like her to look out for them, and I know that the school will feel privileged to have her in post. Thanks also to Jess Fear for her support, and to Julie Monks, our cover illustrator, who took the time to engage in a fine old brainstorm with the group. And last but not least, thanks to my squad of writers: you were awesome. Stick to your guns, and I hope to see you on the other side.

Teacher's Foreword

Sonia Carvill, Librarian and Literacy Manager

We are swimming in troubled waters. Even now, as we seemingly emerge from the worst of the pandemic, there are still casualties, deaths. How hard it has been for adults. How fearful we have been for our children.

At Longcroft, like in all schools across the country, we have seen our mainland school separated into a series of islands, each one a cocoon against Covid, its own outpost. We have felt marooned.

Thank goodness for First Story. Despite the numerous setbacks caused by the pandemic, they eventually arrived, providing a lifeboat in the form of Lee Harrison, our Writer-in-Residence. Lee, laid back, calm and reassuring, has proved himself able to navigate the most unsettling of seas.

When we commenced our voyage, very few of our cohort of Year 8s would have described themselves as writers: 'Miss, I don't know why you picked me to do this, there are much better writers in Year 8 than me.' Reading through the anthology, how glad I am that we did.

At the start of the project there was a lot of coaxing, cajoling, and confidence-building as we convinced our Year 8s that they were capable and worthy of sharing their voices with the wider world. We had a range of abilities, including SEN students with dyslexia and several children from armed forces families – pupils who had travelled the world and knew what it was like to be on an outpost. A huge thank you to Lee for meeting the needs of each pupil and being so flexible in his approach, and to Jessica Fear and the First Story team for their unerring support.

What comes across in these pages is a unique message in a

bottle. Thank you to our Year 8s for their trust and honesty and having the courage to put pen to paper. We laughed and cried, and we learnt from each other.

My grandfather believed the number 8 was special, a number without beginning or end. Let us hope that the confidence our Year 8s have gained on this voyage of discovery remains, and that their belief in their own voices is never-ending. Longcroft is immensely proud of you all.

Outpost 8

Class Poem

We are a small group of troops
Stationed at a distance
From the main body of the army.
Here,
Looking towards the shore,
We are isolated from the world,
Isolated from infinity,
Isolated from our full potential,
Untying the tangle of an impossible knot.

Sometimes, when you leave,
You return to your friends.
Sometimes you don't.
We lost the man, off somewhere
Patrolling to protect our specific piece of land.
We didn't know who he was.
Maybe he was never there.

Being in this family involves moving around,
Making friends around the world.
We feel part of England
Together with friends and family
But I am the #outsider –
A fox-headed pharaoh
Gathering his belongings in jars,
Feeling safer in bed.

The faces –
The voices of friends
Get right on my nerves
But I am grateful for their company.
We are isolated
But we are isolated *together*
And I tell you,
Tall dude, small dude –
We can win the war.

A dirty, burnt sandbank
Slopes down to the river.
On the other side
It is beautiful,
Acacia trees
And rolling mountains
Folded like blankets.

Looking

Rossi Moulson

It was my first birthday
My mum and dad had an argument
I heard the door slam
Dad has gone
He came back five days later
He was looking for something
He wasn't looking for me.

Ice-Lolly

Ruby Stanway

I really wanted an ice-lolly
But my mum said
It's too cold!
So I went upstairs
And put a woolly hat on.

Regeneration

Max Murphy

The neighbourhood was squalid –
Rusty garage doors,
Potholes,
Old cars jacked up,
McDonald's wrappers on the floor.
Council regeneration.
Generations of tenants
Are nostalgic for the past,
The olden days
When the place was box-fresh
And they'll be happy
When they see the past
In front of them.

Safe Space

Henry Tully

When I am not playing rugby
I feel bad,
I feel scared,
I feel shrivelled up.
But after kick-off
When a shoulder hits me like a freight train,
When my nose is mashed into the ground,
I feel fine.
Giving someone a massive hit
Powers my performance.
Kick-off boosts me with adrenaline
And all the pressure drops away.

Military Discount

Isobel Branney

I am an army child.
I've met the Queen –
An experience I'll never forget.
Moving every three years,
It feels like every five minutes,
Walking through a cold new camp, all alone,
Making new friends fast
But losing them in a heartbeat,
Soon being posted to a new country
Which feels like a mystery.
The hide-and-seek games in the mess,
A new dress each year for Remembrance Sunday
Mess dos and fancy dinners
Whilst stealing your mum's makeup
In the painful pack-ups of moving house.
We never got to kick a ball
Across the gigantic gardens,
Never got to repaint
The ugly magnolia, woodchipped walls
But there was money off
The first meal at the Chinese
With military discount.

Greece

Tia Palmer

Greece.
Walking at night on the beach,
Sunset, peach-light sky.
A football field, another summer's night,
Another sunset.
If I was a monkey I could climb trees
Or if I was an elephant I'd have power,
People would listen to me.
I'm safe on a football field,
It gets your head
Out of everything else,
You just think about football,
Your worries go away.
Forget about the family arguments,
Problems with friends,
Just think about football.
Don't do anything wrong.

Last Hopes of a Tree

George Penny

The chainsaw roars.
I begin to fear
My last living breath
Is near.
Chop chop chop, go the human beings.
All I can hope is that I am replaced.
Without me, say goodbye to the human race.
Us trees keep you alive
Taking carbon dioxide
So you can thrive.
Chopping us down
Depletes your oxygen.
Chop chop chop.
Say your final goodbye.

Wing Dings

Arabella Kennedy

The very first thing
I can remember
Is shoving my Tinkerbell
Into a typewriter
Where she lost a wing.
Ding!

Safe Space

Maddison Braithwaite Le Pine

The middle of
Nowhere
Is my safe space.

Rita

Kripa Gurung

In the line for the rollercoaster at Alton Towers, right behind the gate, I saw how fast it took off. When I witnessed this level of speed, my heart was tensing. I could feel the ride, but not my own body. As I sat down on the Rita, I was shaking like never before. I couldn't say a word unless it was to shout, it was so nerve-racking. As I felt the ride push back a little, I heard the words.

Five...

And the first red light went off.

Four...

As another went off.

Three...

Two...

As I closed my eyes, wishing it would stop, I felt like I was going to faint.

One...

My heart raced. There were a million butterflies in my body. Green – and the ride left at the speed of light.

Dance

Laura Campbell

Dance is…
The music in the hall
Blasting through me
The adrenaline coursing
Through my veins
And having that thought
Of never letting go.

Dance is…
My safe place,
The place I feel safest,
The place I feel happiest,
I let go
And dance
Like there is no one else in the room.

Dance is…
The place where all my dreams
Come true
And where new dreams
Are born.

How to Die

Jemma Garnham

Go to the top of a building.
Jump off.
End up landing on a crash mat.
Try to drown yourself.
Discover you are an amazing swimmer and can hold your
    breath for a record-breaking amount of time.
Go to a tree.
Tie a rope to it.
Decide to turn it into a rope swing, with a used car tyre.
Rethink your life decisions.
Go to sleep.

The Sky Splits

Olivia Langdon

The sky splits.

I fall into the dry barren wasteland in single, rounded droplets. They look ecstatic to see me – I must be the first visitor they've had in a while. They dance and clap as I form pools in the cracks in the ground.

Weeks later, I'm almost back home. Most of my kind have fully disappeared, and I'm all that's left of a long, tiresome drought. I evaporate back into the sky, filled with fuels from power plants, waiting for when I'm needed again.

The sky splits.

I fall into the flooded, open wasteland in sheets of droplets. Mud slides, water flows. Now ruined, they no longer look ecstatic to see me. Everything gone, meandering down into dark depths of nothing.

Pieces of Rhyses

Rhys Hodgson

Rhys is aloof, not bothered.
Reese's Pieces is shy.
Rhys's brother calls him Moron.
Idiot.
Reese's-Puffs-viloy is a song that's supposed to be mean.
Rice is the normal me, standing in a corridor
Asking people if they want rice.
Gayboy – ignore, depending.
Greasy-Rhysy-lightly feels as if he wants to punch someone.
Hodgepodge comforts.
Timothy is energised to 120%
Whilst Cici has caring cousins
And whilst CREEPerRhys0908 gasps in hogalouff-Hufflepuff-
amazement
PiePerson3i4
Is recurring…

Carlos the Janitor

Jack Gordon Turner

Carlos the Janitor had a rusty mirror that glowed.
As the glass turned into a door
That led to a land of spin,
With a potion from his scientist uncle
He faced off against a monster made from rust and dust.
Nearer and nearer to his final destination
Carlos lost his mind,
Started to regret his journey.
He felt defeated –
But he drank the potion and suddenly felt strong enough
To defeat the dirty monster, find the diamond mop,
And escape as the cave started collapsing.
He ran for the door,
Treasure in hand,
And never trusted mirrors again.

Crete

Owen Meehan

I remember being in Greece
On the island of Crete.
The sky was bright,
I was in the pool
Swimming
And my parents were on the sunbeds
Burning.

Two 360s

Arabella Kennedy

I was in the car driving down a dirt road in Kenya when my dad tried to swerve away from a pothole.

We did two 360s down the middle of the road, and nearly flipped over and into two Kenyan kids wearing nothing but old clothes and rags.

The dust settled, and they looked at us bewildered, still holding their multi-coloured goats.

How to Be Normal

Maddison Braithwaite Le Pine

Wake up.
Drink something.
Go for a walk.
Put a jacket on and think nothing has happened.
When you see your mates
And they ask if you're OK,
You say yes
And they believe you.

Smudge

Kieran Hope

When I was younger I had a cat called Smudge. She was a black cat with a white chest. She had been run over.

We found a place to dig a grave, but I hit my toe with the shovel. My parents rushed me to the bathroom to put my toe in water. It turned blue for a month.

If Smudge could have seen it, she would have hidden her amusement under the sofa.

Out of the Blue

Ellie Brown

All I wanted was a day to swim freely with my pod. But I had a burden. I swallowed a piece of plastic. I wasn't too bothered with just one bit, but with each metre I went, I could feel my mouth gradually gathering plastic. It became unbearable.

It slowed me down and, steadily dragged off course, I noticed my whole pod was gone. Now separated from my family, the only thing surrounding me was human garbage – bottle lids and balled-up bags, tangled-up mesh and crates. I felt hungry, yet full up on plastic. Every stroke, plastic.

The water became shallower. Out of the blue, I hit the plastic shore. Drained and feeling heavy. I saw humans standing all around me, and I wished I could be free.

Olivia

Olivia Langdon

Olivia
Rhymes with Bolivia
Located in South America.
Olivia Bolivia
Is strong sun-showers,
Empty orchards
And relaxing on the beach abroad.
Sage-green, luscious gardens,
An animal loping
Through tall, sunlit grasses.
But Liv is a perfectionist.
Hardened to gain the respect of others.
Whilst Liv the pianist
Lets loose her façade
And is happiest.

Pivotal Point

Demi Oxley

When I was in my teens
Came a pivotal point.
What do you want to do?
Get into university,
Do a Master's,
Learn more about diversity,
Get a good job,
Earn a promotion fast.
But what do you *want* to do?

I do not want to be an archaeologist
Or a teacher.
I want to photograph the natural world.
Desert landscapes,
The Grand Canyon
And old abandoned buildings
That tell old stories of the circus.

I Remember

Tyla Keenan

Watching TV at my nan's
The phone rang.
Grandad had crashed the car.
I remember
He seemed fine at the time.
But now, I remember
And he forgets.
But he is still determined
To finish his paper round.

Charlie Robinson Has a Motorbike

Charlie Robinson

Charlie Robinson
Has a motorbike.
All day long
He rides it.
Long nights,
Over rocks and bushes,
He never shows his face
And drops in
To see his nana.

Australia

Carmel Woodall

Bondi Beach.
Waves.
Surfboards.
My grandma.

She taught me to surf,
To love dolphins.
She's getting older,
Forgetting things all the time.
She only remembers
Surfing.

I have a scar shaped like a dolphin
And on the beach at night
Looking at the stars
I feel safe.

How I Came to School

Adam Jefferson

I have an uncle who lives in Peru. He owned a pet camel with heart disease. He sent it to me, hoping it would die on the way, as he couldn't bear to be there when it passed away. He'd been given the camel as a first birthday present and they'd spent a long life together.

I rode the camel to school. It did not die. Then I rode it home and it collapsed on the doorstep, and that's why we own a camel-skin rug.

Every time my uncle visits he always avoids the living room where his old friend still lies, draped across the floor.

Soupscape: How to Escape from Prison

Alfie Knight

Finally, it is the day of my execution, so I can get planning for my final escape. My special meal will be a chicken soup.

With just a few drops, I wreck my handcuffs and break out with ease. I move slowly up the ventilation shaft towards the roof. There, I hurry to the rendezvous point, where my friend is waiting in a helicopter. This will take off to Siberia, where I will live the rest of my life in a shack in East Russia.

Dead Duck

Cara Briggs

I was six years old
At my nanny's caravan.
Sat in my pram
Eating a sandwich.
A duck grabbed it.
And in the struggle of trying to get my food back
I accidentally killed it.
I did feel a bit bad
But at the time
I didn't mind
because I had my sandwich back.

Every Two Years

Ella Booth

Ella is
An army child who always moves,
Posted like a letter in the postbox.
She walks through camp all loud and clear
And moves house every two years.
New room,
New stuff,
Must sound fun.

Paphos

Ella Shirt

Meet me in Paphos.
Pelicans to the right,
Restaurants to the left,
Pathway through the middle,
Seafront ahead.

The Problem of Plastic

Rio Keenan

Kim Kardashian was swept into the sea
With all the rubbish
And so began the plastic pollution
Of the ecosystem.

Waterfall

Ellie Allaway

My safe space is the sound of a waterfall.
It calms me when I'm stressed.
The gushing water
Crashing against glistening rocks,
Birds chirping
Beneath the roar,
And the trees
Dancing with the wind.

Shop

Tia Palmer

My dad went to the shops
When I was six.
He's been shopping
For seven years.
Must have been a big shopping list.

Home

Lauren Matthews

My home is listening to music,
It calms me and helps a lot.
Whenever I get the chance
I listen.
Sometimes I think:
How are these people so talented?
It baffles me.

My home is talking and spending time with my mum.
She does so much for me
And will help me with anything.
She is one of the nicest humans ever.
I love her lots and am so grateful she's my mumzy.

Malta

Molly Agus

In Malta, the weather is divine.
The sun feels as if it is right next to me,
Embracing me with a loving hug.
The streets are dead silent
But for the seagulls, begging for steaming fish and chips,
And the water crashing against dusty rocks.
My eyes water in the salty spray.
Meanwhile, the sun heats up the sea, sparkling like a pan of
    water on the stove.

At the Top

Niko Dutkowski

I was made three months early.
I take growth pills.
But they don't work.
They made my baby teeth black.
And I'm still small.
But I climb walls like a lizard.
I am a king, looking down
Like a drainpipe spider,
I creep across the tiles,
I run across the roof
Like a monkey.
The thrill of maybe getting caught
Sends me running
Like a rooftop ninja.
At the top of the Eiffel Tower,
Looking down on my kingdom,
That is my safe space.

Call to Action

Adam Jefferson

Starve the people that are eating the world
Rip their hunger out
Show them what is wrong
They'll only make it worse for themselves
And everyone
Fight them
Make them rage
Impel them to act and show them the right way
You will change the world
For the greater good

Insta Eulogy

Phoebe Smith

When I'm dead
Don't post on Insta
'RIP Phoebe, lost Angel'
Or something like that.
Don't be fake.
To my friends especially:
Don't let that happen.
Make the fakers take it down.
Don't let the bullies pretend we were mates.
If you post about me when I die
And we're not mates
I will haunt you 'til your time comes.
Phoebe XOXO

A Sad Death

Rhys Attwood

Ricky and Freddy
Will never get to do their GCSEs
And you won't get to feel their prickly tongues when they
    lick you
With their lavender scent from the old shack.
They'll never find your scent again
Or get an education
Or have fish and chips,
Whilst they teach you about
The invention of light bulbs
That changed everything.

Last Minute

Rhys Simson

Lock yourself in the tallest building in the world.
It reaches up to the limits of the atmosphere.
Jump off.
Fall until complete.
At the last minute
Ensure you brought a parachute.

Jacob

Keira Jackson

Meet me
When I'm dead.
We'll mess about in the park
Being ghosts in the dark.

Smooth Skin

Ruby Gillyon

I remember swimming with dolphins in Cyprus
In the crystal-clear sea,
Feeling their smooth skin on my fingertips.
I remember the soft seabed,
Shiny, black, leather-covered fish
Among vibrant pink coral.
Hot air against our faces,
Hot sand beneath our feet
And the local men gathered around restaurant tables
Singing in cello-deep Cypriot voices.

Broken Fingers

Henry Tully

Number six stood on my hand
And broke four of my fingers.
These broken fingers once turned purple.
These broken fingers once scored tries.
Once threw rocks into the Humber,
Gave fist bumps,
Dragged me up onto a bin in Oldham,
Wiped tears from my eyes in the final,
Held onto the lead as the dog dragged me through the nettles
Beat my brother at FIFA (12-4).
These broken fingers
Will hold the hands of my grandchildren.
Maybe they'll seize up one day.
But they'll shake the hands of my defeated enemies
And one day lift the cup.

Why Do Cats Purr?

Laura Campbell

Cats purr because they want to start an earthquake.
When enough cats purr
The humans will all be dead
And the world will be taken over by cats.

The Hero's Journey

Owen Meehan

The alarm goes off.
Get out of bed.
My mum puts breakfast in me.
Get changed.
Bike.
Arrive at school.
The hero triumphs.

Kim K

George Penny

Kim Kardashian lives
On a superficial moon
In a cave made of cheese
Looking down
On the barren wasteland
Called Earth.

I Am Glad

Kieran Hope

I am glad I have a fridge
And a family.
I have the right to an education
And Nando's.
And I'm glad I'm in the library right now.

My Favourite Injury

Niko Dutkowski

When my dog
Bit my face
I had to get stitches
And I looked cool.

Magic

Rhys Hodgson

Obviously
I cannot do magic
Otherwise
I would have teleported out
Of this awkward situation.

I Travelled to Turkey

Rossi Moulson

Don't leave your kids like a rat
In a glass elevator.
I would like to be in a hot tub
Next to a psychotic king
On a throne made of quartz.
I'd rather be an eagle
Or a land snail
Than a homeless machine
Broken, old, rotting.
Claustrophobia is like
Crashing into the back
Of my brother's bike.
If I could not see my friends,
I'd rather be a camel
In a pool
Eating waffles
At a gargantuan buffet.
I'd rather build the
World's tallest ice-cream,
Mint choc chip, Toffee
Caramel, Vanilla, Honeycomb,
Than be here in wet, damp England.

Why Do I Feel Dizzy?

Lauren Matthews

I've probably done too much work
Painting my nails for a living
And counting my money.

Bait

Ruby Stanway

It was awful.
There was the hard tough one,
The kind fabulous one,
The faithful but unpopular one.
I had to join the team.
I went to the try-outs
But the whole affair
Was just bait
For humiliation.

School

Rhys Hodgson

School is a military camp
Straight from the Parisian fashion catwalks.
We are baked compliments
By iconic art teachers
And Taylor Swift
Is our headteacher.
I heard that Lady Gaga
Is going to coach the poker team,
Christina Angle-Era is going to be head of Maths
And Celine Dion
Will teach us all about
The *Titanic*.

Invisible People

Olivia Langdon

Every day, invisible people keep ideas
Hidden in important words
Whilst millions of others nearby
Suffer the difficulties and problems
Of real life.

Bones

Maddison Braithwaite Le Pine

The polar bear reminds me of
Bones.
The ice is melting.

How to Use a Pen

Cara Briggs

Pens are used by writers
To stab holes
In the truth.

Rosemary

Carmel Woodall

Spiky and strong,
It smells homely
Like my granny.

Leaves

Maddison Braithwaite Le Pine

Spiky, orange, pretty
Smells like cooking in my grandma's home.
A leaf can have so much history
It reminds me of a new life.

How to Barbecue

Olivia Langdon

Chase cow with flaming torch
And two slices of bread.
Eat your lovely beef.

Bullfighting

Maddison Braithwaite Le Pine

I must say
That I do not admire
The matador.

London

Isobel Branney

I was in London.
Cars racing, birds chirping.
Strolling into King's Cross station
A drunk man was being pinned to the floor
Raging, red-faced, intoxicated.
The police were holding him down.
I felt out of place
Like I didn't belong.

Wrong Plug

Kripa Gurung

I remember when my mum
Switched the oxygen plug
With the vacuum plug.
The fish went
Flopping up and down
As if it was having
A seizure.

Polar Bear

Carmel Woodall

The polar bear is all alone.
It should be on the ice
Looking for seals.
Instead, it is looking
In the bins.

Bookworm

Adam Jefferson

I'm a
Nose-picking
Nail-biting
Book-devouring
Game-playing
Chicken-loving
Film-making
Late-night-reading
Bookworm.

When I'm Dead

Arabella Kennedy

When I'm dead
Burn my body
And scatter my ashes.
But don't take my phone.
I don't want anyone looking at that.

How to Eat a Live Duck

Phoebe Smith

1. Put bread in your mouth
2. Draw the duck in with the bread
3. Wait for it…
4. Grab it by its neck
5. Bite down on the head
6. Eat the rest with no further issues

How to Get a Foot on the Housing Ladder

Rhys Attwood

Get your stuff.
Run to the nearest house.
Wait until night.
Sneak inside.
Grab a weapon and make the owners leave ASAP.
If the police come inside,
Hide, and wait patiently.
Act like a psycho to scare them off.

In Heron Frozen Foods

Arabella Kennedy

Katie spilled
Amelie's newly purchased drink
All over the floor.
Embarrassment spilled
All over her face.

Sun

Jemma Garnham

I walk along the beach,
Warm sand between my toes.
The sun is like
A dandelion.

Obsessed

Ruby Stanway

You used to be bright,
Positive, and relatable
But now you've changed
Since you became obsessed
With Harry Potter.

Wake Up

Jemma Garnham

Beep…
   Beep…
   Beep…
That was all I could hear.

As I opened my eyes, all I could see was a bright light. My eyes stung, but after a few seconds I got used to the glare.

I could see I was in the same hospital room I'd been in before I went to sleep. As I sat up, I noticed that my hair was knotted and messy.

Looking at the clock, I guessed I'd be having my check-up soon. I must have been really tired to sleep all day like that. I waited.

Hours later, I realised the clock hadn't moved. A smell drifted through the open door. Something awful. Something wasn't right here.

I went to the window and opened the blinds, and started to panic.

Over the unlit city, the sky was blood red with black clouds like holes in the world.

Bright Contrast

Ellie Brown

I was named after the Beatles song
But I don't relate to it.
My name is Eleanor,
Yellow and purple
With a fruity taste.
Smells like hazelnuts.
It means bright, shining one,
From the Greek.

Mary, Mother of God

Ellie Brown

The quiet worry of the loud crowd.
My foot stepped into the silence of the aisle.
My heart was thumping.
Walking at pace, I stepped on my dress
And faceplanted the floor.
The loud laughter of the quiet crowd.

Survival

Max Murphy

Survival consists
Of avoiding prey animals
Who are lying in wait.
Since they cannot run
Walruses, seals and sea lions
Lie down and point backwards.

Mussel

Max Murphy

A simple mussel shell
Rough on the outside
Iridescent

Face First

Demi Oxley

My sister stood at the top of the hill.
She got on her bike
And took off,
Flew down,
Reached the bottom,
Fell face first
Into a wooden pole.

Sunflower

Ella Shirt

My grandad deserved the world.
Unexpected death.
We all grieved the loss.
Sitting in his chair,
Looking around the room,
Wondering where his hospital bed had gone.
He never got to watch me grow up.
He never got to set foot outside his
House before his death.
I grieve the loss
Of being his little sunflower.

Dear Unborn Baby

Ella Shirt

You are a month off your due date.
You are the size of a watermelon.
You have the intelligence of a chicken.
But dear unborn baby
I want to tell you that
The world is not at its best at the moment.

Jack Attack

Jack Gordon Turner

My name is Jack.
My name is French.
Jack is the name of a bat.
Bats live in darkness, like me.

Stroking the Cat

Alfie Knight

The cat
Wouldn't let me stroke it
So I put it
In the bin.

Getting Up in the Morning

Demi Oxley

My mum's voice
Trying to do well
Helps me wake

Pheasant

Ella Shirt and Rio Keenan

Learner driver up front.
On the way to the beach
A back-road pheasant
Popped out of the hedge.
The impact of its body
An explosion of feathers
Swirling over the windows of passing cars.
All the way up
To the T-junction.

Endangered

Ella Markillie
Runner up in the First Story EcoPoetry Competition 2021

Those minds are blind. Though they can clearly see:
The warm suffering, the hidden monsters,
The melting future and the roaring pleads.
Though ears can't hear screams, yet they are deafening.
Those eyes are numb. They don't look at their bites.
Nor their scars. Or their guilt. Engraved into hearts.
Then there are other eyes, who feel those wounds
And darkness through the barrel of the gun.

I wish I could make it stop and pause time
But I have not even confessed my crimes.
I may chant a mantra in my mind and
Hold a sign for those eyes for those against us.
But what happens when we realise that
We are those monsters. Are you one of us?

A Melody Lost

Tegan Blake-Barnard
Winner of the First Story 100-Word Story Competition 2021

An abandoned library rests, buried beneath time, watching another sun rise and another day pass. Heavy shelves echo the shades of a shattered grand piano which sulks, heartbroken, by decomposing windows. Reminiscing of a time when each note it sang echoed the whispering calls of vibrant characters snuggled amongst the shelves, when each note clambered over the other in a desperate attempt to harmonise with the whistling birds through the open window. With its back forever facing its audience, its beam-soaked keys embrace the morning sun, the mighty willow giants and the chorus it will never be able to join.

Acknowledgements

Melanie Curtis at Avon DataSet for her overwhelming support for First Story and for giving her time in typesetting this anthology.

Camille Ralphs for copy-editing and Alison Key for proofreading this anthology.

Julie Ann Monks for designing the cover of this anthology.

Foysal Ali at Aquatint for printing this anthology at a discounted rate.

HRH The Duchess of Cornwall, Patron of First Story.

The Founders of First Story:
Katie Waldegrave and William Fiennes.

The Trustees of First Story:
Ed Baden-Powell (chair), Aziz Bawany, Aslan Byrne, Sophie Harrison, Sue Horner, Sarah Marshall, Bobby Nayyar, Jamie Waldegrave and Ella White.

Thanks to our funders:
Amazon Literary Partnership, the Artists' Copyright and Licensing Society, Arts Council England, BBC Children in Need, Fiona Byrd, Beth & Michele Colocci, The Blue Thread, Didymus, the Dulverton Trust, the Garfield Weston Foundation, the Goldsmith's Company Charity, Granta Trust, Jane & Peter Aitken, John R Murray Charitable Trust, Letters Live, Man Charitable Trust, The Mayor's Young Londoners Fund, the Mercers' Company Charity, the Network for Social Change, the Paul Hamlyn Foundation, the Stonegarth Fund, Tim Bevan & Amy Gadney, the Unwin Charitable Trust, the Walcot Foundation, the Whitaker Charitable Trust, the Friends of First Story and our regular supporters, individual donors and those who choose to remain anonymous.

Pro bono supporters and delivery partners including:
Authorfy, BBC Teach, British Library, Cambridge University, Centre for Literacy in Primary Education, Driver Youth Trust, English and Media Centre, Forward Arts Foundation, Greenwich University, Hachette, National Literacy Trust, Penguin Random House and Walker Books.

Most importantly we would like to thank the students, teachers and writers who have worked so hard to make First Story a success this year, as well as the many individuals and organisations (including those who we may have omitted to name) who have given their generous time, support and advice.